I0451678

Partially Broken Never Destroyed 5

The Devil's Advocate

Nataisha T. Hill

Published by TaiLorMade Books

Chapter One

As the sunset began to fade and fluffy pillow clouds traced patches of darkness against the pale blue sky, Kayla sat in the back of her and Bryan's rented limousine watching the wedding party disperse. How could her dream day turn into an unforgettable nightmare? How could she not know as much as she thought she knew about the man she just married? How could she have not taken heed to the signs of Bryan's treachery from the past? He had an affair with a married woman that was her boyfriend's mother for Christ sakes! How could she also had not considered the fact that he secretly had sex with his best friend's girlfriend in addition to being involved in a murder case during his college years? Kayla was heart broken.

Although she had forgiven Bryan for his previous indiscretions, his list of transgressions continued to increase. She didn't know if she was ready or even willing to accept this mystery child that Bryan's cousin claimed he had. Her marriage was ending before it had even begun. Luckily, the tinted windows hid the soaking of her cheeks as she continued to sob the night away.

A few minutes later, the limo door opened and Bryan got in opposite side of Kayla. He rested his elbows on his legs and put his face in his hands. After a long pause, he looked over at Kayla who had positioned her body toward the door and away from him.

"Kayla, I had no intentions of hurting you or letting you find out the way you did. I didn't know about this alleged baby until a couple of days ago. Baby, I'm not sure if it's even mines."

"The fact of the matter is that there is a possibility, Bryan."

"Look, I met Ms. Jenson's niece at that backyard party when I first met you and you were Raymond's girl. That baby has to at least be around two for it to even be a possibility."

Kayla continued to stare out the window as Bryan tried to explain himself. The more he spoke, the more disgusted she became. He had to have been hooking up with her, Jennie, and her niece at the same time at some point. This man didn't only have a closet full of skeletons, but it seemed as if he owned the entire graveyard.

"It seems like every time I forgive you for something, an entirely different situation occurs to where I have to go through the same emotional breakdown all over again. When and where does the chaos stop with you, Bryan?"

"Kayla you are my wife. That means that I chose to be faithful to you and only you under the eyes of God. If I wasn't ready to do that or fully commit to building our lives together, then we wouldn't be here. Do you really think I would deliberately mess up one of the biggest days of our lives by telling you something that I'm not even sure about right before our wedding?"

Kayla turned to look at him, but didn't respond. The look in his eyes said he was sincere, but that wasn't enough. It didn't take away the fact that she not only may have to indirectly deal with Ms. Jenson all over again, but she also had to accept that she wouldn't be Bryan's one and only baby's mother. She knew that her argument would sound selfish to Bryan since he accepted Nicholas as his own, but this was different. Nicholas's dad and his family were nonexistent in Nicholas's life, so they didn't have to deal with custody sharing, weekend visits, or any other drama that could arise with co-parenting. The Jenson family had proven themselves to be demented on several occasions; therefore this niece couldn't be any different. She had to have known Bryan was having an affair with her married aunt.

"We literally just took our vowels for better or for worst under God, and I'm in this for the lifetime haul, Kayla. I need to know if you are, too."

It sickened her even more that Bryan was trying to throw God in the equation to try and minimize his wrong doing. It sickened her to imagine him lovingly holding someone else's baby in his arms. Coincidentally, she started feeling sick altogether. Barely missing her dress, Kayla reached for the door and vomited on the red carpet of the concrete entrance. Bryan immediately ordered the limo driver to take them home.

Still feeling nauseated after arriving home, Kayla took off her wedding dress and showered. Bryan made sure she was okay and told her he was headed back to the venue to make sure they had all of their belongings. After he left, Kayla lied down in the bed and prayed that the alleged baby wasn't Bryan's child. Although he had messed up in the past, Bryan had proven himself to be a great stepdad, lover, and provider. On top of already being married, she definitely didn't want to start over with someone new. She hoped the nightmare would soon end before getting worse. Kayla thoughts were suddenly interrupted by her ringtone. The last thing she wanted to do was talk to someone about her awful wedding reception. She looked at her phone as fear rattled through her bones. Someone was calling from Gabby's phone.

Kayla got up, ran to the bathroom, and vomited again. How and why in the hell would someone be calling from a dead woman's phone? This had to have been some sick joke being played by her boss, Meg. However, from what Kayla had witnessed, Meg was hauled off to jail during the wedding reception. Did Meg really have that much pull to be released that quickly? Besides, Meg was smart enough to know not to use the phone of the person that she helped to murder. Of course, Meg's side lover, Jared Mancini, did all of the physical damage, but Meg was just as guilty by not doing anything and attempting to help hide Gabby's body. To top it all off, when Jared became Kayla's personal attorney, he admitted to her that he was no longer even interested in Meg. Not only had Jared confessed to being gay, but he was planning his life with Meg's husband! Kayla knew that she was intertwined in a twisted situation, but she was not about to further involve herself with this Gabby situation. She wasn't sure if Gabby was alive or dead at this point, but it didn't matter to her either way. There was nothing she could do about something that had already been done. She dismissed the call and immediately turned her cell phone off just in case they continued to call.

Kayla washed up, returned to bed, and rested in a fetal position. She was never going to forgive Bryan or Meg for the anxiety they caused on her wedding day. She was mentally, physically, and emotionally drained from all the events that had taken place. She figured she'd sleep the night away and pray for a better day the next day.

What felt like 30 seconds was about 20 minutes later when Kayla was awakened by a ringing noise. Still slightly unconscious, she grabbed her phone in attempt to stop the ringing, but it continued to get louder and more repetitious. She finally sat up, looked at her phone, and remembered she had turned it off before going to sleep. Still tired, she realized that the ringing was coming from the doorbell downstairs. She lied down again in hopes that the ringing would stop, so she could go back to sleep. Unfortunately, whoever was at the door was very adamant about someone answering it and didn't leave. Her first half-awake thought was that Bryan forgot his keys. He was still being chauffeured by the limo, so he didn't have his garage opener either. In a zombie-like state she got up and walked down the stairs in order to unlock the door for Bryan. Not bothering to look out the peephole, she opened the door and noticed it wasn't

Bryan at all. She was puzzled by what she saw. She was now wide awake and flustered.

"Oh my gosh! What are you doing at my home?"

Chapter two

Bryan slowly walked around the reception room as the janitor swept up left over flower buds and debris from the opposite side of the reception building. The room itself was practically spotless with the exception of a few centerpieces that were left on the tables. Bryan suddenly noticed a half torn wedding program slightly sticking out underneath a tablecloth. He picked it up and sat down cn the chair next to it.

He began to wonder if the broken program was symbolic to his wedding that perhaps shouldn't have happened. Although he loved Kayla, he wasn't quite sure how to move forward if the baby in question belonged to him. He promised himself that he would not allow his future kids to have a broken home like he did. He had it in his mind and heart to make the relationship with his child's mother work out regardless of life's mishaps. However, he definitely didn't expect a child to suddenly appear in his life a few days before his wedding. Deep into his thoughts, a sudden touch on the shoulder from behind startled Bryan.

"Mama, don't be sneaking up on me. I could have accidentally flipped you over from reflexes," he explained, turning to meet her embrace.

"I'm sorry, son. I didn't mean to scare you. I took off my shoes because my feet started hurting from all this walking."

"Mama, you've been here this entire time cleaning up? You didn't have to do that."

"Well, I didn't do that much. They had cleaners come in and do most of the work. I came to get a few things I thought y'all would want so you two could focus on your celebration of love."

"Mama, did we just not witness the same catastrophe that just happened?"

"Listen, son. The devil will pursue you when he knows you're doing the right thing. What you have to do is pray about your situation and cast your cares and worries upon God. Once the devil sees that God has His hands on it, then he will flee."

"Well, Mama, maybe you can explain to me why God brought this unknown baby into our life to stir up strife on my wedding day. You can also explain to me why a good mother like you had to struggle as a single parent while my so-called dad lived the high life."

"Son, I don't blame God for the choices I made and it would be silly if you did. God didn't tell you to go sleep around with a married woman and then trickle down to her niece."

"I know that mama, but I was being immature and having fun. I shouldn't be punished now that I'm doing right."

"Son, you have to be responsible for the seeds you sow and the weeds that came from them. God isn't on our time. In order for you to become a better man, a leader, and a provider, you must own up to your faults and ask for forgiveness. You have to release all that pain and anguish from the past that you subconsciously bring to your present."

"Mama, that's easy to say, but when shit...I mean, stuff keeps happening now, it's hard to see the good in anything."

"Boy, don't you know that God isn't going to set you up for failure. The obstacles in your life are designed to make you wiser, son. What you think is a setback is a setup for something amazing. You need to start being grateful for all your wonderful surroundings. You have a great job, a nice home, and a beautiful wife. You are able to hear, you can see, and you have two legs to walk with."

"Okay, mama, I get it."

"Well, act like it, son. There are people praying everyday to be in your position. If this baby is our baby, then we do what we can to make sure she is happy and loved.

You are officially the leader. Your attitude will reflect how your family responds. I love you, son."

Bryan watched his mom grab the few centerpieces that were left on the tables as she exited the room. He knew his mom was trying to see everything from a positive perspective, but for him, it wasn't reality. His mother was clearly unaware of the viciousness that Mrs. Jenson possessed. It was bad enough that he slept with Jennie Jenson's niece behind her back, but having a baby with her would be the ultimate betrayal. This woman admitted to him that she killed her husband and her own daughter. Therefore, it certainly wouldn't be an issue for her to have her niece and grandniece killed. Knowing this further complicated Bryan's situation. How could he even attempt to build a relationship with this child knowing that she may be a target simply by him being her father? At that moment, he knew he had to figure out a way to make sure that the results came back in his favor. He came up with an idea to pay his cousin Floyd, who looked like him and was around the same age, to take the DNA test for him and use his information.

Meanwhile, back at home, Kayla was dealing with an entirely different issue. She couldn't believe this simpleton, Jared Mancini, had the audacity to show up at her doorstep. She imagined he'd be on the run from killing Gabby, her former colleague. Was he trying to get rid of any witnesses before he left? The entire encounter made her nervous and the look in Jared's eyes made it seem as if he was running out of options. Even though she was slightly terrified, she knew she had to appear as if she was relaxed in his presence not knowing his intentions. She had already made herself vulnerable by opening the door and being face to face with a killer.

"Listen, Jared. If Meg needs bail money, I'm sorry, but I can't help."

"Bail money?" He repeated, seeming to be confused by her statement. "Meg is in jail?"

"Well, isn't that why you're here?"

"Wait, how to you know that Meg is in jail?"

"It's kind of hard to forget when police show up at your wedding and haul someone off in handcuffs in the middle of it."

He took a step back as if all this was new to him. He looked to the right of him as if he was waiting for someone to appear. She wasn't sure what he was thinking, but she knew she had to interrupt the awkward moment.

"Well, I don't expect you to care about my ruined wedding, but I would like to enjoy somewhat of a honeymoon."

"Oh yeah, definitely," he responded, nervously running his hands through his hair. "I'm sorry I disturbed you guys and congrats."

He stumbled a little while walking backwards from the doorway. He continually looked around as if he didn't want anyone to notice him there. Kayla quickly closed the door, locked it, and ran up stairs.

Just as Jared was backing out the driveway, Bryan quickly pulled up and blocked his path. Bryan was very suspicious about this black Lexis leaving from his home. He swiftly hopped out of his car and boldly knocked on Jared's tinted window.

"Oh, hello. You must be Kayla's husband. Congratulations."

"And you are?"

"I'm Kayla's attorney, Jared Mancini. That's my office downtown in the brick square."

"So, why are you here and not there?"

"I'm sorry sir, I didn't mean to impose. Besides this being the weekend, the office is never open this late."

"Listen Sherlock Holmes, I don't give a damn if your building burned down. Don't ever come to my house at night or without my permission, you dig?"

"I understand and I would feel the same way. I just wanted your wife to be aware that it's important not to have any contact with her boss, Meg until further notice."

"So, you couldn't call to tell her that, man?"

"Uhh...I tried, but I guess there was a bad connection."

Bryan suspected it was something fishy about this guy. He took his phone out of his pocket to try and call Kayla. Lucky for Jared, Kayla's phone went to voicemail. Bryan reluctantly went back to his car to let Jared out of the driveway. He pulled into the garage still having an eerie feeling. Kayla had better been ready because she had a lot of explaining to do.

Chapter Three

"What in the hell is this fake ass Antonio Banderas in a suit doing in our home?" Bryan said, forcefully opening the bedroom door.

"Bryan, chill out. He wasn't in our home. He came to the door and gave me information about Meg," Kayla said, sitting on their bed with her arms wrapped around her knees that were cropped up against her chest. She wasn't ready to tell him the whole truth.

"Okay, so you had to turn off your phone in order for your "attorney" to tell you something about your boss?" Bryan suspiciously asked.

"First off, I didn't know he was coming over. I turned my phone off because I was trying to take a nap since I was exhausted from crying all night at my wedding that you and your family ruined."

"Are you messing around with this dude or something?"

"Bryan, Jared is gay. Stop trying to cover up your faults by creating one that doesn't exist."

"I guess he did have a little twang in his voice and I'm not trying to cover anything. I'm just curious to know what was so important that he had to come over at this time of night to tell you to stay away from your boss?"

"He told me Meg found out her husband was cheating, so she tried to kill him. He warned me not to bail her out since Meg came to my wedding directly after the incident. He claimed it could make me look as if I was part of her cover up plan or something. I don't know. I have too much on my mind besides thinking about them."

Kayla knew that she had to remix the story because Bryan probably wouldn't understand or even believe the truth. She could barely even believe the truth and she was a firsthand witness to it all. Besides, she wasn't going to allow Bryan to create distractions from his paternity issue.

"All I know is that you better not let me find out anything different than what you're telling me," threaten Bryan.

"What you need to do is find out if you're the father of that baby."

"And if I am?"

"Then...I don't know."

"What do you mean? We're not dating, Kayla, we're married. You are aware of what vows are, right?"

"Only a person at fault would say that, Bryan."

"No, only a husband who loves and promised his wife forever would say that. I think it's absurd that you're blaming me for this situation."

"No, I blame your ratchet ass cousin and your possible baby momma, too."

"I can't with you tonight, Kayla," explained Bryan as he walked back towards the door.

"What are we going to do about the honeymoon trip?" Kayla asked.

"What are we going to do? What type of silly ass question is that to ask? Are you trying to piss me off?"

"It's not like we're in marital bliss or this 'happy newlywed phase' that normal married couples experience. I'm not trying to fly to the Bahamas to argue, sob, and look out the window all day."

"I know one thing. My money is spent, so I'm getting on that plane with you or without you. Furthermore, I think you're being very selfish and insensitive about the whole situation. I didn't plan to have my first child with another woman and it isn't my fault it all came out the way it did. I need your support more than ever right now."

"Goodnight, Bryan," Kayla said as she tucked herself under the covers.

Bryan shook his head, walked out of the room, and slammed the door. He was hurt that Kayla would have the nerve to question their marriage over something beyond his control. After accepting and treating Nicolas as if he was his own son, he couldn't believe that Kayla wouldn't do the same for him. Although he didn't necessarily want the kid, he definitely expected his wife's loyalty and understanding of the circumstances. He certainly had been faithful to her for at least the last two years, so that should count for something.

While walking downstairs to grab a beer from the refrigerator, Bryan got a call from Wayne.

"What's going on, bruh?"

"Bryan, man, you have to help me."

"Help you on my wedding night, man, are you kidding?"

"This is serious, Bryan, I really need you on this."

"Help you do what, dude?"

"Jesse is flipping out about this Justice situation. She keeps making threats to disappear if I don't tell her the truth and all this other bullshit."

"Okay, so how does your mess involve me?"

"I had to tell her it was you that dated her sister."

"Wait a minute. You told your girl whose sister was murdered that I dated her? Have you lost your damn mind? I have enough problems on my own right now. I'm trying to get my own marriage on track. I can't get involved with any other nonsense."

"Bryan, this is not nonsense. I really do love this girl. Besides, Jesse knows you ain't no killer. I didn't say you were involved with her death; I just said you dated her."

"Wayne, you should've thought about this mess before getting mixed up with her sister. I told you back then I didn't want anything to do with this mystery girl and I especially don't want anything to do with it now."

"I told you I didn't know they were sisters, dog. Besides, if your girl hadn't said anything to Jesse about Justice, we wouldn't be having this conversation."

"No, if it wasn't for your dumbass having weed and a gun in the car, we wouldn't have gotten arrested in the first place and I wouldn't have to have explained to my woman why an investigation was being done."

"You couldn't just lie and say it was the gun and weed charge instead of bringing up shit we did in college?"

"Wayne, I don't know what type of girls you deal with, but Kayla is by far not a dummy."

"What does that suppose to mean? Are you trying to insult my woman?"

"What I'm trying to do is not get involved in your relationship point blank period."

There was a moment of silence. "Listen Bryan," Wayne said, lowering his tone, 'I'm really trying to do right by this girl. I'm just asking for a tiny favor from you to help me make this right."

"Man, I personally don't care what you tell her, but I'm not cosigning on shit if she ask. I can't believe out of all the dudes we use to hang with back in the day, you didn't bother to give her anybody else's name."

"When Jesse asked me why did Kayla tell her I was being investigated about Justice, I had to say you were hiding shit from Kayla, so you put it off on me."

"That's silly as hell, dude."

"It just made sense at the time. So, if she asks you did you-"

"Wayne, I'm NOT getting involved with that nonsense, man,' stressed Bryan, now aggravated.

"Alright, forget it then and congratulations on your love life since that's the only one you're worried about."

Bryan hung up even more frustrated than earlier. He refused to agree to have messed around with someone he hadn't ever met. Although Wayne still didn't know, he was already sleeping with Jesse back then. If he lied and told Jesse that he was also sleeping with her sister, she'd really go nuts. Besides, what type of best man would try to get him involved in some bullshit on his wedding night? Wayne was too immature and from the looks of it, he was never going to change. Bryan made a decision to slowly cut Wayne off completely.

Chapter four

Kayla woke up late the next day feeling drained from all of her sobbing episodes. Bryan wasn't lying next to her, so she assumed he had slept on the couch or in the guest room. *Well, this is a great way to start our marriage*, she thought. She wasn't sure what she was going to do for the next few days since she still had two weeks off from work and three days until the honeymoon trip. Nicholas was going to stay with his cousins until they got back from the honeymoon trip that Kayla wasn't even certain if she was still going to attend. While washing up, she began to think more about what happened at her wedding. She wondered was she being selfish by not trying to see things from Bryan's perspective. From what she gathered, the baby was almost two, which meant he dealt with Jennie's niece almost three years ago. Even though it didn't excuse his promiscuity, it wasn't Bryan's fault that this chick decided to come out the shadows after all this time. The more Kayla thought about it, the more she realized she was being completely irrational. She went downstairs in her robe to find Bryan who was sleeping on the couch with his arm covering his face.

"Are you asleep?" She asked.

"I guess if I was, you were going to make sure I wasn't," he responded.

"I want us to talk, Bryan."

"Do you want us to talk or for me to listen to you tell me how I've ruined our marriage?"

"Listen, I know I've said some harsh things, but I've been doing some thinking."

"We both know your way of thinking is what really counts in this relationship."

"Could you stop being so damn sarcastic for one second and listen?"

"I'm listening."

"I was a little over sensitive about the baby thing. Everything that has taken place lately has my mind and emotions in a hundred different places. I guess I was just crazy about the idea that I would eventually be your one and only baby mother, but either way, I don't want to argue anymore. Let's just do what we have to do and move forward."

He reached out his arm for her to come to him. She quickly accepted his invitation as he embraced her through her robe. He whispered how much he loved her as he wrapped his arms around her naked torso and softly began caressing her back. He sent chills down her spine and her hormones became raging with sexual anticipation. She removed her robe and allowed him to fondle her breast. She took off her panties and climbed on top of him, wildly sucking and licking his lips as she waited for him to remove his briefs. He slowly slid his manhood inside of her with a deep thrust. With one hand gripping her hair and the other gripping her buttocks, he synced his stroke with the squeezing of her booty each time he penetrated inside her. Paralyzed by his stroking action, her body tensed up as she felt her sexual orgasm rapidly building. She aggressively grabbed his neck as she increased her up and down momentum. Moments later, she released a loud, gratifying moan as he finished and shook himself inside of her. Kayla wasn't sure if it was the psychological reaction of knowing that their union had been blessed or if her hormones were out of control, but she felt as if she had just experience the best climax ever.

Although a huge weight had been figuratively lifted from her shoulders, Kayla was physically exhausted. She returned upstairs for a quick wash up and decided to lie across the bed for a quick snooze. As soon as she closed her eyes, her phone rang.

"I just want a nap," answered Kayla, annoyed and unaware of who she was speaking with on the other end.

"A nap? What are you, pregnant or something? It's almost one in the afternoon."

"Oh my gosh, it's you. What do you want, Meg?"

"Now is that any way to speak to your boss and good friend?"

"You're a devil in a dress. Whose phone are you calling from?"

"You and I both know that's not important, dear. Listen, I need you to meet me for a late lunch at Joe's Crab Shack around two thirty."

"You're kidding, right? My attorney, also known as your lover boy, advised me not to have any contact with you."

"Kayla, we must not speak of dialogue from fairytales over the phone. I know you're on a temporary leave, but there are some important documents that we have to discuss before you return to work. I'll see you in a bit."

Kayla immediately hung up and threw her phone on the bed. She was pissed at herself for even answering the phone. The last thing she wanted to do was deal with this dangerous adulteress. She knew Meg didn't have any important documents to discuss, but what other choice did she have other than to meet with this woman. Meg was still head of the nursing program and had the power to terminate her. Kayla hated the fact that a devious person like Meg was in control of her career. She needed Meg fired from her position and out of her life for good. She knew that she had to think of something to turn the tables.

Still lying down contemplating her next move, Bryan came in the room and sat down next to her. He fixed a portion of misplaced hair from her face and began caressing her back. His comforting touch put her back into relaxation mode.

"Wow, I didn't know my lovin' could make your skin glow so beautifully."

"Are you ever going to stop being so conceited?" Kayla asked while giggling.

"Isn't being conceited how I got you in the first place?"

"No, actually it was your humor."

"Girl stop. You know good and well you couldn't resist my swag game."

"I can't with you right now, Mr. Swag."

"Yeah okay. Maybe not right now, but we have each other forever."

"Yes, we do," she said, rising up to meet his kiss.

"Listen baby. If I haven't said so already; I am truly sorry about how things turned out at the reception and for getting us into this type of predicament. As much as I don't want this to be my child, I'm truly blessed to have you on board and by my side regardless of the results."

"I guess I forgive you," she teased. "Even though we had started dating around that time; we weren't exclusive, so I guess I will also admit to overreacting just a little."

"Baby, I could never be mad at you for your emotions. It's my cousin who I'm pissed at. That damn trash should have at least kept her mouth shut until our celebration was done. It really wasn't her place to say anything period. Her trifling ass not going to do anything for the baby even if it is mines."

"Well, maybe someday soon she will admit she was wrong."

"Trust me, baby, that will never happen. Anyway, I'm about to go and holla at Wayne. He said he forgot to give us the Dom Pérignon that he had gotten us for our wedding. He said it's for our honeymoon trip, but we can open it tonight if you'd like."

"Did he really forget to give it to you or was he just upset because I had Jesse escorted off the premises?"

"He didn't mention it, so I don't know."

Bryan suddenly realized that Kayla probably was the reason Jesse had gotten all fired up again. Even though Jesse had no right to disrespect Kayla in their home a few weeks back, Kayla shouldn't have blurted out details of the private conversation he had with her. Bryan definitely had no intentions admitting it to Wayne, but Kayla played a key role in opening Pandora's Box.

"I think I should get a pregnancy test," Kayla blurted.

"Where did that come from?"

"Uh...just being tired and moody," she said, not wanting to tell him that Meg put the thought in her mind or the fact that she spoke to Meg period.

"Babe, you're always tired and moody because of your long work hours. Then, there's added stress with your boss and everything that happened at the wedding."

"Are you trying to make me not pregnant or something? I haven't been at work in almost two weeks and I doubt if Meg is making me vomit."

"What? You just said you needed a pregnancy test, but now you're talking as if you know you're pregnant."

"I'm just saying that you sound as if you'll be disappointed if I am pregnant by trying to create ways that I'm not."

"You know what? You might be pregnant because you just went from ten to a hundred in three seconds. I'm going to leave and I'll get a test while I'm out," he said, kissing her on the forehead and exiting.

Kayla felt frustrated all over again. Not once did Bryan say he'd be thrilled if she was carrying their baby. They were married, so she expected at least a small reaction of excitement from him. She got up, got dressed, and decided she was going to get a test herself. She just hoped this meeting with Meg wouldn't be a catastrophe.

Chapter 5

On the way over to Wayne's crib, Bryan couldn't help but to
wonder was Kayla really pregnant. A part of him was happy that he
may be having his first official seed with his wife. Kayla was a great
mother and he had definitely grown to love Nicholas, but this would
be his first opportunity to raise a newborn baby. The fact that his
own dad wasn't around made him that much more adamant to be a
great father to his children. He knew he was financially stable
enough to raise a child and his mom would be ecstatic, but he also
had his reservations. Having his former fling niece's child in
question was overwhelming. Bryan felt like he would become a
father of three overnight. Although Kayla said she would be
supportive, Bryan was still thinking of getting his cousin to take the
paternity test with Jennie's niece for him. He didn't want any
dealings whatsoever with the Jensons and with the possibility of
Kayla being pregnant; it was almost as if it was his only option.

Bryan pulled up to Wayne's new home, turned off the ignition, and sat there for a minute. He remembered where the house was since Wayne had drove them there the day of Wayne's closing. He hadn't been inside and was now having second thoughts about being there. He'd been dealing with Wayne's stupidity for years, but he definitely had no intentions of putting up with his disrespectful broad. All the things that went on over six years ago was old news, so if Jesse brought it up, that's exactly what he was going to say.

"Hey, what's going on my guy?" Wayne asked as he opened the door for Bryan.

"Man, nothing much. Thanking God I got through this wedding ordeal," Bryan responded, sitting down on the living room sofa.

Much to Bryan's surprise, Wayne had the front of the home looking nice. He had a huge leather sectional with a flat screen mounted over an in-wall fireplace. The floor plan was open, so he could also see the nice granite countertops and updated appliances in the kitchen.

"I know right. What was up with ya cousin snapping off the way she did?" Wayne asked, grabbing the remote as he reclined.

"That was crazy, wasn't it? I guess Renee still blames me for losing her baby when James went to prison. I'm the one who told James dumbass not to go and get that dope from them that night."

"Yeah, I remember that because they tried to rob him. He shot like two people that night didn't he?"

"Yeah, but one died like two weeks later. They got him on a couple of charges."

"Why is she mad at you, though? You're the one who warned him."

"She's mad at me because I originally said I would go with James to meet them to make sure everything went as planned. They called James the night before the meeting day and told him to come that night to their spot. I told him that wasn't the plan and something sounded fishy. He said I was a money hater, so he went solo."

"That's messed up though. Greed changed the course of his whole life."

"It's beginning to affect mines, too."

"Is Kayla tripping or something?"

"Wayne, what kind of question is that? My cousin just told my wife that I have a baby she doesn't know about."

"I see ya point. Is it yours?"

"Man, I don't know. At the reception, Renee said the little girl is sixteen months, which would make it impossible for me to be the daddy. I went to see the baby the night before the wedding, and the baby's mother said she was twenty-two months."

"That's a big damn difference. Someone gotta be lying."

"I know. I really need to see a birth certificate before I even consider taking a test."

"Did you tell Kayla that you went to see the baby?"

"Hell yeah. I didn't have any other choice."

"Ha ha ha. I bet she flipped out on yo ass, too. Kayla be looking mean as hell sometimes."

"Oh, don't act like Jesse didn't put one across yo head yesterday by the way you were crying and asking me to lie for you and shit."

"Whatever, man." Wayne said and laughed. "Man, all women crazy."

"You ain't never lied."

A few minutes later Jesse walked through the door with a few shopping bags and a weird expression on her face. She walked past the guys without saying anything. It was almost as if she didn't even notice they were there.

"See man, I told you," Wayne said, shaking his head at her antics.

Jesse returned moments later and sat her purse on the table. She went into the kitchen, grabbed a beer from the refrigerator, and sat with the guys.

"Dang, babe. You couldn't grab us a beer?" Wayne asked.

"You two were sitting here before I was, so you could have gotten your own beer."

"That's what I be talking about right there. I gotta go get my guy his champagne bottle anyway, I'll grab them."

"The wedding was nice, Bryan. I'm glad I could attend," Jesse said after sitting in silence for a minute.

"Oh. Thanks," Bryan replied.

"I was obviously being sarcastic."

"Well, thank you anyways."

"Here you go, my guy," Wayne said, returning with a beer and the Dom Perignon.

"I think you two are really meant for one another. You both think you're more than what you are," Jesse continued.

"Jesse, I don't mind you chilling with us, but there's no need to disrespect my company."

"I'm not being disrespectful. I'm just telling him the truth. Him and his uppity bitch belong together."

Bryan wasn't sure exactly what Wayne told this chick, but it was clear to him that she was ready to get something off her chest. He could have been petty and called her out for all the recent attempts she made to get with him, but that would put him in a two against one situation. He didn't want to get the bottle and run, but that's exactly what he planned to do if Wayne didn't put a muzzle on his chick.

"I'm not the smartest guy alive, but I'm starting to think you want Bryan or something. Why are you all up in their relationship and shit?" Wayne asked Jesse.

"Oh, so now you're trying to take his side when you just told me last night that he was a dog ass nigga who took advantage of my sister."

"Okay, but whatever he had with your sister was between them and quite frankly, that still doesn't have anything to do with you."

The room became so quiet that you could probably hear a heartbeat. Although Bryan still didn't appreciate the fact that Wayne lied about him dating Justice, he had mad props for him putting Jesse in check. It was about time he showed her who wore the pants. He decided this may be the perfect time to excuse himself.

"I am so sick and tired of you assholes thinking that the fuckin' world revolves around you," Jesse said, getting up walking back toward the kitchen.

"Ain't nobody in this house holding you hostage and you know where the damn door is," expressed Wayne, unable to hide his annoyance.

"Okay. I see what this is. Y'all punk ass niggas think y'all about to gang up on me, huh?"

"Bryan and I were having a man to man conversation until you came in acting like a ratchet bitch."

"I'm with a bitch ass nigga, so what do you expect?"

"Jesse, I'm done. Get your shit and go," Wayne demanded.

"Wait. I know you're not kicking me out of our house."

"Jesse, you know good and damn well you haven't paid a dime toward this house."

"I can't believe you would do this to me in front of this nothing ass boy!" Jesse screamed, gesturing toward Bryan who remained silent.

"Maybe it's because I'm with a nothing ass girl," Wayne said.

"I trusted you, Wayne. I thought you were different. You're just as disrespectful as your little friend over here. I'm beginning to think...maybe you both had something to do with my sister's murder."

Wayne laughed. "You're fucking psycho," he said as Bryan lightly giggled along with him.

"I guess you guys think I'm a joke, huh?" Jesse asked, retrieving a gun from her purse.

"Oh shit!" The guys shouted.

"That's right. Oh shit. Now, I want some fucking answers. Who killed my sister?"

Chapter six

Kayla arrived at the restaurant about 10 minutes after the time she agreed to meet Meg. She was hoping Meg had already left, so she could have a legitimate excuse to leave. Much to her dismay, she noticed Meg's car parked out front. Since it was obvious that Meg wanted her to know she was present, she got out of her car and tried to think of an excuse to make the meeting as brief as possible. She figured she'd tell Meg that she had a meeting with her travel agent regarding her honeymoon. Besides Meg's face being the last face she wanted to see, she began feeling nauseated again. It had then dawned on Kayla that she agreed to meet Meg at one of the most odor lingering restaurants on the planet. She walked in and the smell of seafood consumed her. She quickly ran to the bathroom and vomited in the stall.

After getting herself together, Kayla spotted Meg sitting at an outside table with sunglasses on, a straw hat, and a flower sundress. Her long, brunette hair was lightly blowing in the gentle breeze as if she was in a Pantene hair commercial. Kayla thought her outside appearance was very fitting for the devil in disguise.

"Hello Kayla. Wow. You look...flustered." Meg said as Kayla sat down at the table.

"Hello Meg. You look like you're auditioning for the remake of the Pretty Woman movie. Done any sex scenes with Richard Gere lately?" She teased.

"Whoa. It seems like you just inconspicuously called me a whore, but it's such a beautiful day that it doesn't even matter. How are you, Hun?"

"I'd be a lot better if I knew why I was here and when I can leave."

"Kayla, you're so cute when you're agitated. How far along are you, Sweetie?"

"What? I'm not pregnant."

"Of course you are. I've been in healthcare too long not to know these things."

"I'm not pregnant." Kayla firmly stated.

"You're in denial, Sweetie, and when you are ready, we can talk about it. Now, getting to the point of why I called you here is because we're in trouble."

"Here is your Moët, Ms. Wright," interrupted the waiter, handing Meg her glass. "What can I get for you, ma'am?"

"Oh, just water." Kayla responded, anxious for the waiter to exit.

"Make sure this section is closed off, Sweetie," Meg demanded, also making sure he was out of sight.

"What do you mean we?" Kayla continued.

"I mean you and me. I got the word from an acquaintance that Jared is trying to pen Gabby's murder on us," Meg whispered.

"You must mean he's trying to pen it on you. Jared knows I had nothing to do with that and so do you. I wasn't even there when it happened. There's absolutely nothing that could link me to that. Besides, I thought you two were in love. Why would he pen a murder on you?"

"Of course you were there, Honey. Jared invited us outside right after the incident. It was your advice to keep the plastic off her face."

"You know what the hell I mean, Megan. I didn't take part in any of that. I was there to get my account straight."

"The jury won't believe that, dear. You don't think that the fact that Gabby screwed around with your boyfriend and you having an extra hundred thousand in your account would link you to a murder?"

"He was my ex-boyfriend at the time, Gabby was married, and I gave that money to a charity."

Meg laughed. "You can't think I'm foolish enough to think you gave that much money to a charity."

"You still didn't answer my question. Why would the love of your life try to send you off to prison?"

Meg paused. "There's someone else."

"What do you mean?" Kayla asked as if she didn't already know that Jared was gay and sleeping with Meg's husband.

"I'm in love with someone else. I have finally found my soul mate."

"Wait. What? How many people are you sleeping with?"

"How dare you turn up your nose at me when your husband is creating kids that you don't know about. That's right. A mutual acquaintance that was in attendance told me about what happened when I left."

"Oh, you mean when you were escorted out by the cops."

"Kayla, don't ever compare your life with my life. I'm rich."

"You're miserable." Kayla challenged.

"Actually, I am in a great place. I worked things out with my soon to be ex-husband, and I feel complete with my current situation, but there's just one problem. We have to get rid of Jared."

"What in the hell is wrong with you? What do you mean get rid of Jared?"

"I mean exactly what I said. He is a potential threat to our future and we must not have loose ends."

"Meg, you are crazy! I'm not helping you do something like that."

"All I need for you to do is convince him to meet you at a secluded place that he will be comfortable enough to agree to. My people will handle the rest."

"You really are the devil. I'm not doing that. I'm not your flunky. He was your lover. I'm sure you can find some way to lure him into your trap. I'm not going to hell for you."

"Kayla, I'm sure we're on the same hell bound list. You're just a few pages down. You know if you refuse to help me I'm going to need that money back."

"Even if I had the money; I wouldn't give it back. You don't get a two for one deal. You're lucky I haven't turned you both in to the authorities."

"You really are in denial," Meg said as she laughed, "How many times do I have to tell you no one will believe you over us."

"You really think so, huh? Maybe that would be true if Jared hadn't come to visit me last night."

Meg nearly spit out her champagne from the comment. By that time the waiter came back out with Kayla's water as Meg stared at Kayla with a look of anger and defeat. There was a moment of silence as if they were trying to read each other's thoughts.

"You're lying," Meg said with a smirk.

"He did, which is how I know you're not as powerful as you think you are. As a matter of fact, he advised that I stay clear of you, but I came here to get your side of the story since you were so adamant about me coming. I must say his version was much more convincing."

"You two can't plot against me. I'll have you both begging for mercy."

"Yeah. He also told me you'd try to make threats, but to allow him and your 'soon to be ex-husband' to handle it."

"My husband?" Meg questioned, looking around in confusion.

Kayla knew that she was embellishing the truth, but she had no other choice. She still had every single penny of the $100,000 and she wasn't about to allow Meg to get her hands back on it. Meg knew that by Kayla having that money, her losing her job at the hospital wasn't something Meg could blackmail her with. On top of that, if Kayla was pregnant, having the money would offer that much more stability. Kayla knew that she had to do some additional quick scheming since this psychotic woman was obviously planning a hit out on her former secret lover and maybe her, too. Kayla wanted to tell Meg that her husband was sleeping with Jared to stir up things even more, but she couldn't. Not only would Meg not believe her, but as vicious as Meg was, she'd probably find a way to make Jared and Mr. Wright turn their wrath towards her. She needed them all to war with each other in order to eliminate herself from their twisted lives.

"It's been nice, Meg, but I have to run. Good luck with your new relationship."

"Kayla, this isn't over," chimed Meg as Kayla walked back into the restaurant.

Once Kayla made it to her car, she had to put a part two into play. She took a few minutes to think about what she was going to say before calling Jared. She played out a few scenarios in her mind until she came up with something that she felt would get Jared's blood boiling. She reached into her purse and dialed his number, hoping that she wouldn't get his voicemail.

"Hello Ms. McQueen. What can I help you with?"

"How dare you come to my house and put on this fake ass show," Kayla said, pretending to be angry.

"Are you sure you dialed the right number?" Jared asked.

"I would think so. What other man would pretend as if he didn't know his adulteress was in jail when he had already bailed her out. What was the purpose of you coming to my house? Were you trying to extort information from me?"

"Kayla, I have no earthly idea what you're talking about. What kind of information would I be at liberty to extort from you that I didn't have the resources to obtain on my own?"

"This is almost unbelievable. You two really are two of a kind. I spoke with Meg already, Jared. I asked her why did the cops come and pick her up at my wedding. She told me not to worry about it because you guys were practically making love in the back seat before they could even get her booked."

Kayla wasn't sure about the nature of Meg's new relationship, but she had to again embellish what Meg had told her. Knowing Meg, Kayla's version of events probably wasn't too far from the truth. Her only objective was to let Jared know that Meg had someone else, without directly telling him. The fact that Jared had himself moved on in a foul way had no bearing on Meg's betrayal. In hindsight, he had actually killed for this woman. Jared didn't say anything, but his silence said enough. No man likes to be played even if he is doing his own dirt. Kayla wasn't sure what was going through Jared's mind at that time, but the seed had definitely been planted. She told Jared that she was done with his lies and Meg's arrogance. She hung up before he could say a word. Having a small inkling that her plan could backfire, Kayla took a breath and left the parking lot.

Before heading home, Kayla grabbed a pregnancy test from the drugstore. Even though she had told Meg she wasn't pregnant for her own protection, Kayla had a gut feeling that she was. She went in the house, put her purse on the bed, and went directly to the bathroom. She went over the instructions, preceded with the test, and anxiously waited for the results. Kayla heard her phone ringing from the bedroom and went to answer it.

"Kayla this is Wayne," he said in a crackled voice. "I can't believe I'm telling you this but…Bryan's been shot."

Chapter seven

Kayla couldn't breathe as she immediately burst into tears. She felt like her heart was falling from her chest. There was no way this could be happening. She had just married him yesterday, there's no way he could be shot! A part of her wanted to think this was a sick joke, but she could hear in Wayne's voice that it wasn't. Besides the fact that Wayne had never called her phone a day in his life, she knew it was real when Wayne repeatedly began apologizing. He proceeded to let Kayla know what hospital they had taken Bryan to and that Bryan was responsive until he was taken away in the ambulance. Kayla had a hundred questions to asked Wayne, but the agony inside left her speechless. Where was he shot? How did it happen, but more importantly, who did it? Unfortunately, those questions would temporarily remain unanswered. Wayne immediately hung up the phone.

After calling her mom, Kayla quickly packed a few belongings and headed to the hospital. She wasn't sure how fast she was going, but minutes felt like hours. Her hopes were that the bullet had grazed his arm or something that wouldn't cause permanent damage. In order to maintain the small amount of self-control that remained, she had to talk herself through the best case scenario of what she was about to encounter.

After rushing through the emergency entrance, it was obvious to Kayla that she was the last person contacted. Bryan's mother was there and a few other out-of-town family members that hadn't left after the wedding. As soon as Kayla made it over to their area, Ms. Irene walked up and embraced her.

"He's going to be okay, baby," she whispered.

"What are the doctors saying? Is he okay? Can I go see him?" Kayla asked, almost breathless and bombarding Ms. Irene with questions.

Darren, one of Bryan's cousins, grabbed Kayla's arm. "I think you need to take a few steps back, calm down, and stop acting like a damn maniac," he said.

Kayla didn't understand. She never had a problem with Darren. She had just met him a week prior to the wedding. She couldn't quite grasp what was going on until she turned and saw Renee giggling in a corner seat. Kayla's worry quickly transformed into uncontrollable anger. It could have been her hormones, Bryan's paternity situation, Meg's bullshit, or the fact that her new husband was in the emergency room that completely pushed her over the edge. It was too late to turn back. The beast had been shaken and awakened.

"Get out of my face!" She screamed, grabbing and twisting Darren's arm as she forcefully shoved him into the nearest wall. Kayla then ran towards Renee, but other family members rushed in and grabbed her.

"Don't hold her. Let her go," said Renee, now riled up with Kayla.

"Bitch, I will knock the entire top row of your teeth out of your mouth," threatened Kayla.

"The top row out of your mouth," repeated Renee in a taunting manner. "Real bitches don't talk proper, hoe. You ain't bout it, bitch."

"Excuse me, you guys are causing a disturbance and you're going to have to leave before I call security," warned a nurse.

"Renee, please leave. You've done enough," spoke Irene.

"Auntie, are you seriously taking her side?"

"My son is fighting for his life and this is his wife."

"She tried to attack me," argued Renee.

"Your attempt to think smart has you acting dumb. I overheard you and Darren's conversation before Kayla even got here. I've asked you nicely once to leave. I will not ask again."

Renee immediately walked out and so did Darren. Although Kayla's intuition was accurate, she now felt ashamed. She acted a fool in front of her mother-in-law who had to have been just as worried and afraid as she was. She turned to the nurse and to her mother-in-law and began apologizing as she wailed in tears. Ms. Irene explained to the nurse who Kayla was and that she was also a fellow head nurse at their sister hospital. The nurse showed

43

compassion as she began to express her sympathy. She promised to keep them updated on Bryan's condition.

After sitting there for a few hours, Kayla's phone continuously rang. She finally had to put it on vibrate to stop the annoyance. She assumed that everyone probably thought it was people trying to call and check on Bryan, so no one questioned her. However, that was far from the truth. Kayla was ignoring those calls for a totally different reason. She knew there could only be one reason for the repetitive calls. Jared must have come for Meg about the conversation they had and now Meg was coming for her.

Attempting to keep their minds occupied, Irene told Kayla several stories about Bryan when he was a kid. Kayla learned that even as a child, Bryan was charming enough to talk his way out of being punished at school as well as at home. A few of the other family members that were also still there laughed and chimed in on their childhood antics. Kayla momentarily forgot about her issues and enjoyed the family connection. The moment was short-lived when a doctor walked around the corner. He asked to speak to the wife in private, but Kayla grabbed Ms. Irene's hand and they followed him around the corner.

"There were a few obstacles; however, we were able to successfully remove the bullet. Mr. Phillips lost a lot of blood, so there is a possibility that he may need a blood transfusion."

"Can we see him?" Kayla asked.

"He's not quite conscious yet, but they are setting him up in a room that will allow two visitors at a time. Now, we normally try to obtain blood from family members since members of the family are normally compatible unless disease stricken or pregnant. Do you know someone in the family we could test?"

"Uhh...We just got married yesterday, so this type of discussion hadn't presented itself," Kayla nervously responded.

"Wow! That's awful. I'm sorry to hear that. Well, we can test you first if you'd like and then move forward to other members if you aren't a match," suggested the doctor.

Kayla looked at Ms. Irene who seemed puzzled by Kayla's hesitation.

"I'm not sure if...if I'm going to be a good fit."

"Oh, that's no problem. Our test will be able to confirm that."

"No, that's not what I mean. What I'm trying to say is...that I may be pregnant," she finally admitted.

"Oh. Wow. Well, we could have you tested for that too while you're here if you'd like," he offered.

Kayla felt as if her back was against the wall. She knew if she took the test there, it would be a big possibility that Meg could discover her results since news always spread quickly to their sister hospital. Ms Irene had already told the nurse who Kayla was and where she worked. However, if she didn't take the pregnancy test, it would seem as if she didn't want to help her husband or maybe she was connected to the shooting. Now that she thought about it, where in the hell was Wayne?

"Doctor, I'm sorry to change the subject, but what part of his body was my husband shot?"

"Oh, forgive me. I was under the impression you were aware. He was shot about six inches away from his heart. A few inches closer would have killed him instantaneously."

"Excuse me again, but why would you be under the impression that I knew?"

"The detective said that the patient's wife reported the shooting."

At that moment the doctor was paged and he excused himself. Kayla turned to Ms. Irene who seemed just as confused as she was.

"I don't understand what's going on? Who called you?" Kayla asked Ms. Irene.

"Wayne."

"What did he say?"

"He said that you said there had been an accident and Bryan was on his way to the emergency room."

"That is ridiculous! Are you serious? Is there any reason no one thought to call and confirm this with me?" Kayla couldn't escape her fury. She was about to explode yet again.

"We were just thinking of Bryan, so there really wasn't time to question it," explained Irene.

"First off, I would have been in the ambulance with my husband and not arriving here after his entire family. Second of all, Wayne would be the very last person I would have called. Wayne called me while I was at home trying to take a pregnancy test. Bryan was with him!"

Irene had an expression on her face that Kayla had never seen. It was a look of complete anguish. Irene walked around the corner as Kayla followed. She began mumbling something that Kayla couldn't understand. Irene grabbed her pursed and frantically began searching for her phone. Her family noticed that something was wrong and began to try to console her.

"Auntie, what's going on?" One of the nephews asked.

Ms. Irene didn't respond. It was like she was in a trance. She walked over to the corner of the waiting room and made a call. Kayla heard Ms. Irene speaking a language she didn't understand. The family then began swarming around her like worker bees protecting the queen. Kayla was confused by the chaotic moment.

"She's speaking French," a cousin finally said to Kayla.

"Okay, but what is all this? Why is everyone swarming around her?"

The cousin got up and walked toward Kayla. "This means *somebody* has to die," she whispered and joined the family.

Chapter Eight

Kayla watched as the family continued to huddle and speak a language she couldn't understand. She had no idea that Ms. Irene could even speak French. Did that mean that Bryan could speak French as well and had been hiding it from her the entire relationship? Who did she really marry and what kind of family secrets was he holding? It started to make sense as to why his family was so scattered and why Renee seemed so withdrawn. Kayla had so many questions, but the last thing she wanted was to get answers she wasn't ready for. For all she knew the cousin could have been trying to scare her. Surely, his family probably still assumed she had something to do with the shooting since they had gotten a bogus report earlier from Wayne. Besides, the Irene she knew was a gentle-hearted woman with unconditional love, so at that point, Kayla decided to ignore the cousin's comment. She put in her mind that the language and the family swarm was a traditional way of them dealing with tragedy. They were simply praying for the best outcome.

Shortly after the incident, a nurse came out and informed Kayla that she and one other family member could visit Bryan in his room. The nurse also advised them that Bryan was still unconscious, but there may be a possibility that he was aware of their presence. Kayla thanked the nurse for her positive outlook and took a deep breath as they followed her down the hall. She wasn't sure if she was prepared to see Bryan in such a vulnerable position. He was always so spontaneous and energetic. He was the one who picked her up when she was feeling down, so she felt as if she had no one to turn to. Bryan meant the world to her and the thought of losing him was unbearable.

"It's okay, sweetheart. God is going to take care of everything. Stop worrying so much," whispered Ms. Irene, grabbing Kayla hand as if she read her thoughts.

They quietly entered into the room as if they were trying to prevent a newborn from awakening. Much to Kayla's surprise, he actually looked as if he was simply sleeping aside from the IV running through his arm. She glanced at Ms. Irene who had the same hopeful look in her eyes. She eased up to him and gently grabbed his hand. It actually felt warm, which gave her even more comfort. Leaning over his body, she gave him a soft kiss on the lips. She looked at him, hoping that maybe he would grab her hand and squeeze it back. She wanted to believe that the nurse was right and that he would feel their presence. Her hopes and expectations quickly began to fade. With the exception of him breathing, Bryan didn't move. He laid there stiff as cardboard and Kayla couldn't take it.

"I want them dead," Kayla said, beginning to cry.

Irene walked over to Kayla and put her arm around Kayla's waist. "Listen baby, if you're more caught up by the wickedness and evil of this world, then guess what, you're going to live in and around hopelessness and despair. But, when you allow the beauty and mercifulness of God's everlasting grace to overshadow the hurt and negativity that you've endured, then and only then, will you live in the abundance of His glory."

"Ms. Irene, I understand the wisdom in your words, but it doesn't stop the pain in my heart. I want my husband to be able to hear me. I want him to be able to speak to me. I just want my husband back."

"My words won't stop the hurt, but God's aid will. You have to trust and believe in the process."

Ms. Irene moved closer to Bryan, "I love you, son," she said as she kissed him on the forehead, hugged Kayla, and left the room.

Kayla was moved by Ms. Irene's encouraging words. What she said totally contradicted the insinuation that Ms. Irene had just put a hit out on someone. Kayla couldn't understand why Bryan's cousins were so hostile and conniving. It made her that much more thankful that the majority of Bryan's relatives lived in other states.

As the night passed, Kayla sat to the side as family members alternated Irene's visitor pass. Most of them didn't say much, but a few whispered something to Bryan in secrecy before leaving the room. Ms. Irene had brought Kayla a sandwich and chips from the cafeteria after each family member had their chance to see Bryan.

Kayla was suddenly startled and almost choked once she heard Bryan coughing.

She opened the door and yelled, "Nurse!" Not knowing what to do. A younger black nurse in her mid 20s quickly walked in to assess what was happening. She must have been on graveyard duty because this was the first time she'd entered the room. After checking his vitals and breathing, she hooked up the oxygen equipment on the side of his bed and placed the mask on his face.

"No worries. He's doing fine. His body is in great condition. It was probably just a brief obstruction, but we're going to put the oxygen mask back on overnight. It's just a precaution since the injury was so close to his lungs."

"Thank You," Kayla said, slightly relieved.

"Visiting hours are over at eight, but you two can stay a little longer if you'd like."

"Oh, I'm his wife and I'm here all night, but mom is going home."

"I'm sorry if you were misinformed, but no one is allowed to stay overnight in any part of the intensive care unit unless you are a doctor or nurse."

"Well, I'm actually the head nurse at our sister hospital," Kayla mentioned.

"Well, unless you have some overnight transfer papers on the way and an assigned shift, you won't be staying here."

"Someone should give you a lesson in common decency young lady,"

Ms. Irene added.

"Be that as it may, you ladies have about forty-five minutes and don't worry, I'll take good care of Bryan," the nurse mischievously said, walking out of the room.

What did she mean his body is in great condition and she'd take good care of him Kayla thought? It was obvious to her that this nurse had a little crush on her incapacitated husband. It also became apparent that the nurses had to have been discussing Bryan in order for her to know him by name.

"I don't trust her," Ms. Irene said, "We can't leave our Bryan alone with her."

Kayla being over protective and possessive of Bryan was normal, but Ms. Irene being bothered by the nurse's presence took the situation to another level. Kayla wasn't comfortable leaving her husband around thirsty nurses in his condition. She had no clue of the nurse's intentions. Her thoughts ran wild as she imagined the nurse giving Bryan an erection and riding him while he was still unconscious. Her thoughts grew even more erotic when she imagined the rest of the graveyard nurse's joining in to get their turn. *What if one of them got pregnant during the madness*? Kayla was in a deranged state of mind. All the chaos that had taken place overpowered her rational thinking.

Kayla walked out of the room and went to the nurse's station. She needed the name of the nurse who was working Bryan's area. No one was present at that time, but she was obviously aware of where they kept the log in information. She walked around the counter and quickly grabbed the chart. Just as quickly as she grabbed it, she almost dropped it. Kayla felt as if she was about to have a nervous breakdown. There was no way she was reading what she thought she had read. Her head began to spin as she tried to take it all in her brain. It could have been a coincidence, but more than likely it wasn't. It was then Kayla realized that the only way Bryan and her had a chance at true happiness was to get away and move out of town. The people who Kayla and Bryan were associated with were evil. Not only were they evil, but they also had a ring of evil connections. Kayla stood there in disbelief that the nurse's name was Jasmine Jenson. She theorized that Jasmine Jenson could be no other than a relative of Jennie and Jackie Jenson.

Chapter nine

Kayla's thoughts were tumbling in a hundred different directions. She wondered if Jennie Jenson had somehow found out about the shooting or if her niece, Jackie was trying to get a swab for the paternity test. Perhaps Jennie wanted to hurt Bryan because she found out that the marriage was official or even worse, maybe she heard that Bryan got her niece pregnant. With all the possibilities, Kayla knew she had to pull some serious strings and she had to do it fast. Even though she hadn't confirmed that the nurse was a relative of Jennie Jenson; she was not about to sit around and wait for something to happen. Even if she couldn't break their policy and stay with Bryan overnight; she at least needed Jasmine Jenson as far away from Bryan as possible. There was only one person who she knew who could pull off this request. She would have to break down and consult with Meg, her demon boss in human disguise.

Kayla got on the elevator and went outside to have some privacy. She thought about how she was going to approach the conversation since she obviously had ignored Meg's calls earlier. She knew that Meg wasn't going to do anything out of the kindness of her dark heart, especially if Jared had spilled the beans about what she told him earlier regarding Meg's new lover. She had to find a way to compromise with Meg in order to get what she needed done, which possibly meant revealing Jared's secret affair with Meg's husband, Dylan Wright. With no other readily available alternatives, she dialed Meg's number.

"I tried to call you earlier to give you some essential information regarding your life, but now (sigh) I'm not sure if I want to share any of my knowledge with you," said Meg, not wasting time with a formal hello.

"I think me being here for my husband is more important than anything at the moment," Kayla responded.

It was clear to Kayla that Meg hadn't spoke to Jared. Otherwise, Meg's first words would have been full of anger and threats. If by chance they did speak, he likely just asked questions to compare stories. Jared prided himself on being the greatest attorney in town. Knowing Jared, he was busy trying to leak Meg's extra infidelity to her husband. Regardless of Jared's agenda, Kayla had an objective. She decided this would be the perfect time to manipulate Meg into believing that she was on her side before Jared made his move.

"Oh yes, I heard about your husband's mishap. I also called you to give my condolences," Meg added.

"I definitely appreciate it, Meg. Going through something like this has helped me to realize who really cares for me. I have to admit that you're the first person aside from my family to tell me that. I apologize for being so hard on you earlier."

"Well Dear, I've told you a dozen times I'm on your side. Just like today, this imposter at the police station was pretending to be you and I had to put a stop to the foolery."

"Wait...come again?"

"I left my Berlin Gucci wallet down at the police station and so happened, when I returned to retrieve it, some girl was pretending to be you. It was a shit show in there. That's how I found out your husband was shot."

"Did you get her name? How did she look?"

"I don't know. She was small with curly hair. I told the officer who I was and showed him a picture of us we took a few months back. The girl at the station claimed that she didn't have any identification on her, so they held her at the station. I'm not sure what happened next because I left."

It all started to make sense. Wayne and Jesse were trying to cover for each other. One of them shot Bryan. Although Wayne was an asshole at times, he didn't have the heart to shoot someone. Besides, Wayne was Bryan's best man, so it kind of eliminated him. All signs pointed to Jesse as the shooter. However, Wayne trying to cover for Jesse made him just as guilty.

"Listen Meg. I need you to do me a small favor. The nurse's here are incompetent, so I am asking if you have the authority to send the graveyard nurse's from our sister hospital to look after

Bryan. This way, I don't have to hang around here making sure things are handled properly. This will free up time that you and I can have to focus on how we're going to work things out with Jared and for me to find my impersonator."

Kayla had become pretty good at fast-talking her way in and out of situations with Meg. She figured she'd put everything out at once and use the new information Meg gave her, so she wouldn't sound calculated. This way, Meg wouldn't have time to consider if there were other ulterior motives. She also didn't want to lay things on too thick, so she waited for Meg to respond.

"Yes, I will do it right now, so we can meet and make some arrangements tonight."

It was an unexpected request that Kayla had to agree to. She knew that Meg would not follow through with her request if she didn't agree to another meeting. Kayla had yet again put herself in a compromising situation. She had to find a way to get out of participating in the planning of Jared's murder.

Against her better judgment, Kayla made plans to meet up with Meg once again. Her main objective was to get that transfer done, but she also didn't want to discuss anything incriminating over the phone. She still hadn't come up with an idea to eliminate herself from partaking in Meg's criminal masterminding, but she had to put that issue to the side for the moment. She returned to the room for her last 30 minutes or so to be with Bryan. Even though he was still unconscious, she still wanted him to feel her presence. Meg bringing in nurses that they knew and worked with helped calm her nerves and since Meg was making the call immediately, the nurse's should be switched out by the time she left. Being on call the first few years of her career, Kayla knew that nurses didn't get much time to drop everything that they were doing and get to work.

As time passed, visiting hours were almost over and there were no new nurses that came in to introduce themselves. Before leaving, Kayla and Ms. Irene promised Bryan that they'd see him tomorrow as Kayla left another gentle kiss on his lips. Ms. Irene had caught a ride with her family members which left Kayla time to see what was going on with the nurse transfer.

She wandered around until she found the head nurse's office and was politely greeted by an older Puerto Rican woman in her late 50s. Kayla explained who she was and her reason for being there. She also told her where she worked and provided her badge as confirmation for her visit. The nurse seemed pleased to meet her and invited her in the office. She introduced herself as Isabella Martinez and motioned her to have a seat.

"I'm so sorry for what you're going through," Isabella said in her lovely accent.

"Thank you. This was definitely unexpected being the day after our wedding," mentioned Kayla as her voice cracked.

"Oh my goodness, no! I'm so sorry," responded Isabella, reaching out to hug Kayla.

Isabella was very personable and she had a great spirit. The last thing Kayla wanted to do was unintentionally insult her leadership regarding her graveyard shift nurses. She had to think of something clever.

"I don't mean to intrude like this, but my boss, Meg Wright said she would be calling you to replace your nurses with our nurses. I told her it was totally unnecessary, but she was very persistent and said she knew what was best."

"Yes, I know Meg Wright. She is very meticulous that lady, no?"

Isabella's demeanor changed. She could tell that Isabella knew Meg from personal experience by her expression at the mentioning of Meg's name. Although Isabella remained professional, Kayla could tell that her encounter with Meg wasn't pleasant.

"Oh, I take it you've worked with her at our sister hospital," Kayla asked, trying not to be intrusive.

"We were on the same committee at one point of time. If she calls, I'll be sure to let her know I'll personally watch over your husband for you. Hopefully, he will be well and stable before a transfer could even take place."

"She said she would have the nurses here tonight, which is why I came to you. I know Meg can be notorious at blind-siding others when she wants something done her way."

"Even with my approval it would at least take three business days for a transfer to take place."

"I must admit that Meg had me under the impression the transfer was best, but now that I've personally met you, I know he's in good hands."

"Oh thank you, Señorita. I will personally make sure of it."

Kayla spoke with Isabella a little while longer about her and Bryan before departing from the office. She felt confident that

Isabella wouldn't allow anything unprofessional to take place. At that point, it wasn't as if she had any other option. On the other hand, Meg had another thing coming for deceiving her yet again. Meg knew she was lying when she said that she could get the transfer done that night. According to Isabella, Meg hadn't even made the call. This was it for Kayla. She and Meg were done. She mentally proclaimed an all out war against her boss.

Chapter Ten

Once again, Kayla sat in her car to decide how she was going to handle Meg. She knew if she confronted Meg with the information that Isabella gave her, she would simply deny it or say Isabella rejected her request. No matter how Kayla would've presented it, Meg surely would have found a way to turn things around in her favor. Knowing this, Kayla had to do something drastic. Her first thought was to continue what she started earlier. She decided it was time for Meg and Jared to see each other face-to-face.

"I'm starting to think you're stalking me," Jared sarcastically said as he answered Kayla's call.

"Don't flatter yourself, I prefer straight men. Anyway, I didn't call to discuss my sexual preference. I have information for you that I will not discuss over the phone."

"Why would you call me about something you can't discuss over the phone?"

"Meet me in the Hilton Hotel parking lot in thirty minutes.'

What an asshole Kayla thought, immediately hanging up knowing he would take the bait. She also wanted him to meet her at the Hilton because that's where Bryan's cousins were staying. She definitely didn't trust Jared and she knew he was dangerous. She was going to lie and tell one of Bryan's cousins to sit in the car to ensure everything went well as she tried to retrieve money from a person who owed Bryan.

About 35 minutes later Kayla sat in the car with Bryan's cousin outside of the hotel. With the exception of the incident that Kayla had with Darren earlier, Bryan's other cousins were supportive and protective. To Kayla's surprise, an additional cousin volunteered to sit in the back seat. Perhaps after discovering that Kayla wasn't involved in Bryan's shooting, they accepted her as family. They made a few jokes about memories they had with Bryan, but they also asked quite a few questions about Bryan's friendship with Wayne. A few minutes later, Jared pulled up in his Lexus.

Kayla got out the car and told them she would be right back. As she walked over towards Jared's vehicle, she noticed him squinting his eyes as if he was trying to see who was in her car. Kayla was humored by his curiosity.

"Don't worry they aren't here for you. We're headed out of town to continue our wedding celebration," Kayla said, leaning into Jared's passenger window.

"Yeah, sure, so what do you want?" He asked as if he didn't believe her.

"It's not really what I want, Jared. It's about what I don't want to be involved with."

"Listen, tell me what you need to tell me or else I'm leaving," he threatened, changing his gear.

It was obvious to Kayla that Jared was intimidated. Even though he had been around Kayla several times, he clearly didn't expect her extra muscle. He may have even assumed that he was about to get jumped or robbed.

"Okay, I just thought you'd like to be the first to know about a hit being put out on you, jackass."

"You can't be serious. Why would anyone even think that would be possible?"

"Anything is possible when you're trying to pin a murder on your ex lover to live happily ever after with her husband."

Now having his undivided attention, Jared put his car back in park. He tapped his fist against his mouth and blankly stared out the window. There were situations in life where there wasn't a turn back moment. This was definitely one of those instances.

"Look, I have to go. The last thing I want my family to assume is that we're over here having a lover's quarrel, but I will leave you with this confidential information. I'm not meeting Meg at midnight behind your office where your cameras are not functional."

Jared looked at her as if she gave him the final piece of validity that he needed. Kayla knew that Jared would not only know that the camera ordeal was something only Meg could have revealed, but also that Meg was willing to leak things he told her confidentially. As Kayla walked off, she didn't feel good or bad about her conspiring. In her mind, evil with evil yielded more evil, but evil against evil ultimately created a fight for domination.

Kayla finally went home to get some things together for the next few days. She didn't want to be home alone, so she considered staying at Ms. Irene's home. When she went in her bathroom to pack a few necessities, she noticed the pregnancy test still sitting on the counter. She walked over and saw Pregnant on the stick. Kayla sat down and thought about the possibilities of her being pregnant dealing with Meg. For the sake of her family, she had to do something. She needed some type of strong evidence against Meg.

About an hour had passed as the midnight sky produced a misty fog and scattered clouds covered the moonlight's brilliance. The night was grim and everything was as still as standing water. Kayla parked Bryan's Hummer out of view adjacent to Jared's attorney office to satisfy her curiosity of what would transpire between Meg and Jared. She knew she wouldn't be able to hear anything from her position, so she made a plan. Dressed in all black, with a black baseball cap and black boots, Kayla found a shadowy area behind a group of bushes and small trees to hide. She was going to record what Meg and Jared were saying, so she have something concrete to use against them if they tried to reverse things and drag her into Gabby's murder.

It wasn't long before Meg showed up and parked behind Jared's office. She saw Meg shaking her head and moving her lips as if she was annoyed that Kayla wasn't already there waiting on her. A few minutes later an unfamiliar car pulled in and parked in front of Meg's car. Kayla knew it had to be Jared because he was the only other person who knew about the meeting. Meg stepped out of her car as if she recognized that it was Jared. Kayla immediately started recording.

"Jared, what the hell are you doing here?"

"You tell me, Meg. Why are you having meetings in the back of my office?"

"I don't have to answer to you. You're not my dad or my husband."

"Meg, you don't have a husband, remember? You're screwing me and God only knows who else."

"You listen to me, Jared. You and your dad still owe me from that jam I got you both out of when that whorish mother of yours tried to take everything your dad had."

"Kayla was right. You really are delusional."

"I could care less about what you or that little bitch has to say. You should have taken care of her when you took care of Gabby. You're too damn incompetent and you leave too many loose ends."

"I'm sure you didn't plan this secret meeting with Kayla to tell her how much of a bitch she is."

"Don't you worry about how I handle Kayla since your sensitive ass couldn't get the job done."

"What did you call me?"

"You're sensitive and weak like your father," repeated Meg, pulling a cigarette from her purse.

"Dylan doesn't think I'm sensitive."

"That's because he thinks you're a charity case. You're like the homeless son he never had."

The moment grew silent. Jared leaned against his vehicle with his arms folded. From the way this conversation was going, Kayla knew that Jared was about to expose his relationship with Dylan. Lucky for her, she'd have it all on video.

"He respects me more than you think and we're actually great friends."

"He's your mentor. Of course you'd feel that way. Him giving you guidance is like him feeding a stray dog. It keeps him grounded."

"You're actually the bitch and you had a different tune when I was feeding you my penis."

"Jared, I'm totally done with you and I have moved on to something better. Lose my number and stop calling my husband for advice. Your services are no longer required," Meg said as she walked away from him.

"Dylan will always require my services," bragged Jared.

Meg turned around and slowly walked back towards him. Even from a short distance, Kayla could see her disgust.

"You two are lovers?" Meg asked, mortified by her own realization.

"The best there is," he confirmed while winking and smirking.

"How long has this been going on?"

"It's been going on long and hard for quite some time," he snickered.

Before Jared was able to react, Meg reached in her purse and promptly slit his throat. Jared grabbed his throat with a look of shock as he slowly fell to the pavement. The moment seemed nothing short of a movie scene. It was the most gruesome thing that Kayla had ever witnessed.

Chapter Eleven

Kayla continued to watch the horrific incident unfolding right in front of her video camera. Although it was obvious that Meg didn't plan to kill Jared, her demeanor definitely wasn't apologetic. She wasn't flustered or panicked. She actually relit her cigarette and started smoking with one arm folded, holding up the other. She briefly looked around, got in her car, and just sat in it. Kayla couldn't tell if Meg was trying to get caught or if she had completely gone insane. Kayla stopped recording when she saw Meg hit the steering wheel. Perhaps there was an ounce of decency left in that tiny heart of hers. Kayla knew she couldn't leave until Meg left. As Kayla remained in place, she couldn't help but to wonder what was Meg doing with a blade in her purse? She was the one who was supposed to be meeting her. Was that blade intended for her? Just then, Kayla's phone rang. Meg was calling her.

Kayla quickly silenced her phone as she watched Meg call back to back. She saw Meg hit her steering wheel several more times after each call went unanswered. Kayla had every intention of talking to her, just not at that moment. Meg finally pulled off from the parking lot and Kayla was able to return to the Hummer. Kayla still couldn't fathom what just happened. Meg killed the man she was having sex with in cold blood. Never in a million years did Kayla expect that to happen. She began to cry at the fact of how her life drastically changed in the course of two days.

With Jared's dead body still lying on the concrete across the street, Kayla knew she had to make a move. Although the area was dark and secluded, it was only a matter of time before someone spotted the ghastly crime scene. Meg clearly became a raging nut case and Kayla knew she was out for revenge. Kayla also knew she couldn't go home or to Ms. Irene's house. Instead, she decided to check in a hotel near the hospital.

Still having anxiety over what she just witnessed, Kayla peeped out the curtains to see if Meg had possibly caught her and trailed her there. After looking at an empty parking lot for several minutes, Kayla went to shower. She thought about all that was going on and how she wanted to disappear for a while. Besides the fact that she didn't want to leave her family or cause Nicolas any instability, Bryan's recovery could take weeks or even months. She wondered how she was going to deal with all the drama and have a healthy pregnancy. Bryan was down and out, so she felt as if there was no one there to protect her. At that moment, Kayla knew it was time to stop sulking and take charge for the sake of her family and the new baby. It was time to make this tragedy work in her favor. She was going to do so with the video she had recorded.

After getting herself together and rehearsing her conversation with Meg, Kayla thought about taking a small drink from the mini bar, but she quickly came to her senses. She went ahead and made the call to Meg from the hotel while blocking the number. Being that it was late and around 45 minutes after the incident, Meg would probably assume it was her.

"This better not be who I fucking think it is," Meg threatened.

"You seem upset. Did something happen?" Kayla antagonized, sipping a drink of water.

"You little bitch. You have no idea what I've been through. You will pay for standing me up and creating the mess you've made."

"I figured it was about time that you and Jared talked since you two had been having some miscommunication lately. How did it go?"

"Listen here you little cunt. I don't have time for these games. I am rich. Don't you know I have the power to destroy you and everyone around you that you love?"

"It's interesting that you say that, but I have a better idea. How about from now on you address me as your majesty."

"You can go to hell."

"Wow, such harsh words. I'm only kidding, but Mrs. Phillips would be nice."

"If you continue to play with me, I will have your husband's balls sliced off, wrapped up, and I will personally hand them to you."

"Okay, now you just sound plain bitter and psychotic. I'm going to record the rest of our conversation and call my attorney to let him know you're threatening me and my family."

As much as Kayla hated to admit it, she enjoyed getting Meg all riled up and their verbal jousting match. She also took small pleasure in knowing that she was about to take Meg's arrogance and figuratively shove it down her throat. It was just like Meg to try and find a scapegoat for her actions, but Kayla wasn't having it. True enough it was her who told Jared about the meeting, but she didn't put the blade in Meg's hand and make her use it.

"I am your attorney and your worse nightmare. You just wait," Meg shrilled.

"Meg, it sounds like you're still threatening me. You should calm down and watch what you say over the phone."

"This isn't a threat, Kayla, and I'm glad you're so enthusiastic. I'm going to wipe that pretty little smile right off of your face. I am promising you that your entire family will look over their shoulders for the rest of their natural lives. That's 'if' Bryan survives."

"Now, now Meg. There's no need for that. I just call to check on you and tell you about my most recent experience. I was walking through the park and the outskirts of the general area. I must say I caught this amazing little video," Kayla said, sending the footage to Meg's phone.

"Wh...wh...what...how...?" Meg stuttered, obviously speechless.

"I've allowed you to carry on enough. Not controlling yourself is how you got in this mess in the first place. I've already sent this special little video to a very secret and special person. If anything happens to me or anyone around me, I gave specific instructions for this video to go viral. If I break a nail in your presence, you'd better be on the phone setting me up with the top manicurist in town."

"Kayla, I am so sorry. I didn't mean to. It was an accident," claimed Meg, wailing in defeat.

"You don't have to explain it to me. That's between you and whatever gods you serve."

"How dare you share something like this outside of our pact? I would never do this to you. I've treated you like nothing less than a daughter."

"What in the hell is wrong with you? You talk as if you just didn't threaten to cut my husband's balls off."

"I am distraught, Kayla. Can't you see that?"

"I see that you're in a very uncompromising position and you'll say anything that favors you."

"What do you want, Kayla? You're heart is just as wicked as mines. You obviously set the stage for what happened to happen and then you had the audacity to record it. If you want money, I have money and millions of it in our private account."

"Meg, I'm not in to the blackmail thing. All I want is you out of my personal life for good. I understand that we have to momentarily work together, but let's make any work-related business that we have to share as brief as possible."

"But would if I get caught or something happens to you beyond my control?"

"I guess you better make sure I have a wonderful life."

"What do you mean? I'm not God. I can't guarantee that."

"You're actually the opposite of God. He gives life and you just took a life."

"Kayla, you are my only friend and I need you more than anything right now."

"Meg, you made your own bed, so you have to deal with lying in it. You also should ask yourself why you planned to meet me knowing that you had a blade in your purse."

Meg not giving an answer led Kayla to further assume that she was correct. It was obvious that Meg wasn't going to admit that the blade was intended for her. She literally held Meg's fate in her hands and Meg knew it.

"It's been a fun ride Meg, but here's where I get off. Good luck."

Chapter Twelve

Kayla couldn't sleep due to the constant nightmares she had about Jared. She didn't even turn on the television because she knew every local channel would be discussing the dead body of a prominent attorney that was found downtown. Kayla contemplated whether or not she was going to release the video to authorities despite what she told Meg. Although she managed to put on a strong front while on the phone last night, Kayla felt terrible about the entire ordeal. Jared had his asshole ways, but never in a million years did she think Meg would have slit his throat. She also figured the police would question her once they checked Jared's cell phone records, which kind of made her nervous. However, the police knew that Jared was her attorney from the day he rescued her from the police station regarding her ex roommate's murder case. The irony in this case was that her rescuer was deceased and she was the only person who could bring him justice by turning in his murderer.

After leaving the hotel room, Kayla's first priority was to check on Bryan. Before she could even make it to the hospital, the local radio station was blasting Jared's death. She turned it only to hear another radio channel broadcasting Jared's dad ranting about a full blown investigation. With all the news coverage, Kayla wasn't going to have to turn Meg in; the investigators were going to sniff her out like a blood hound. Kayla turned on her music player to avoid what she thought were constant reminders of what she needed to do.

Once Kayla arrived at the hospital, she checked her face in the mirror. She knew she looked pale and worn out, but she wanted to be the first person Bryan saw when he opened his eyes. She put on her sunglasses to prevent everyone from noticing the exhaustion on her face. As soon as she walked through the visitors doors, she was greeted by an unlikely guest.

"Hey Kayla, I've been waiting on you to get here," Meg whispered.

"You've got thirty seconds before I unleash hell," Kayla said.

"Please, just listen. I want to talk to you outside."

Hesitantly turning around, Kayla walked back out of the doors, "What do you want?"

"I wanted you to know that I called in the best doctors there are to assist with Bryan."

"Wow, you learned my husband's name. Is that all?"

"Listen, I know this is an awkward situation, but I was hoping we could still build our relationship and get back to how we use to be."

"My focus is on building my husband back up during his recovery. Good bye, Meg.'

"Kayla wait. One more thing before you leave. I know you seem to be a moral person and all, but there's something you should know about Jared."

"Do you really think it matters at this point?"

"He was planning to pin Gabby's murder on you, Kayla. Gabby's missing body, the call from Gabby's phone, and him showing up at your house was his entire insane plot to pin the murder on you. He was going to plant evidence in your backyard and call the police, but his plans were halted when Bryan came home."

Kayla knew Meg was a liar, but there was truth to her story. The only way Meg would know those details is if Jared told her. It was just a pity that Meg would try to put everything on a dead man who couldn't speak for himself. Kayla was well aware that Meg wanted her to disappear as well. The fact that Meg would try to make it seem like she did Kayla a favor by killing Jared was yet another insult. Kayla pulled out her phone to find the portion of the video where Meg called her a bitch and said that Jared was too weak to get rid of her. She played it out loud for Meg and watched the shameless look on Meg's face.

"Kayla, put that thing away," Meg whispered in a panicky voice.

Kayla took a step back and looked at Meg's made up face, fashionable dress, and Red Bottom shoes. Whatever event that had taken place and whoever was involved in creating this monster was tragic. There was no hope for this lady and Kayla knew it. She had no morsel of a guilty conscience about anything she had done. She was literally her own destruction.

"This is your last warning. Stay away from me and my family," Kayla said, walking back into the hospital.

Kayla went into the bathroom and applied a little powder and eyeliner to her face before seeing Bryan. If she learned anything at all from Meg, it was to look your best even when things around you were a disaster. Once Kayla made it to Bryan's floor, she was politely greeted by the nurses and even a few doctors called her by name. She wasn't sure if this was Meg's doing or Isabella keeping her word. Kayla opened the door and nearly fell out.

"Hey beautiful lady!"

Kayla immediately started crying as she walked over to Bryan. Seeing him sitting up and conscious elated her spirit. She sat on the bed, held him tightly, and didn't let go.

"Baby, it's okay. I'm okay. Everything is going to be alright," he said, holding her face.

"Why didn't you call me when you woke up?"

"I knew you would be here as early as possible and a hundred different specialists and doctors have been in here, so I really didn't have time."

"How do you feel? Are you breathing okay? What did the doctors say?"

"Baby, I'm fine. The doctors said I'm a medical miracle and I'm healing at a rapid rate."

"Well, that's perfect because we're going to need you around for your son or daughter."

"Are you serious, baby? You're pregnant?" Bryan excitedly asked.

"Yes. You're going to officially be a dad."

"It's amazing how the worse moment of my life just became the best. Now, all I have to do is take this damn paternity test, so we can move on with our lives."

"I know right, but don't you worry about all that right now. We just need you healthy. So, how did this happen?"

"I was chilling at Wayne's crib. Jesse came in and started talking about her sister's death and pulled out a gun on me and Wayne. Wayne got up, called her a stupid bitch, and tried to grab the gun. They started screaming at one another, so I got up and started making my way towards the door. The last thing I heard was Jesse saying 'it ain't even loaded' and then lights out for me. I really couldn't tell you who shot me."

"We were told you were shot in the chest."

"No. The bullet came in from my back and went through my chest."

"Well, dumb and dumber are both guilty. Wayne is guilty for lying and telling the police you were with me when you got shot and Jesse's dumbass went down to the police station pretending to be me."

"I don't know, babe. They were probably just scared and didn't know what to do or say. I think it was an accident."

"That's no excuse. Grown people shouldn't play with guns. You should have seen what happened when Ms. Irene found out that Wayne lied to her."

"What do you mean?"

"She and the family huddled and started speaking French or something."

Bryan had a mortified look on his face. He immediately asked for his cell phone that the nurses had given to Kayla. He tried to get up, but he was still weak from the shooting.

"Baby, relax. What's going on? Why are you so fidgety?"

"Kayla, you don't understand."

A nurse walked in and told Bryan that they had to do more testing before they could release him out of ICU. She also told him they were moving his room to the general area where Kayla could stay with him all night. They advised Kayla to wait in the waiting area for about an hour until they could run the test and get Bryan transitioned.

Kayla followed their instructions and headed towards the waiting area on the floor of Bryan's new room. She wasn't sure who Bryan was trying to call and why he became so panicky. She was still emotional and excited to see her husband alive and awake. Now that Meg wouldn't further intervene in her personal life, she could focus on her new marriage and her pregnancy. Kayla also hoped that Bryan would exclude Wayne from his life, but that idea was probably a far shot since Bryan felt it was an accident. Deciding not to over think things, she remembered Ms. Irene's words about just relaxing and trusting the process.

About twenty minutes later still sitting in the waiting room, Kayla began texting a few of Bryan's cousins to let them know he was conscious. She didn't get any response, so she figured they were sleep or either getting ready to start their day. She had already called Ms. Irene who said that she would be coming later in the afternoon. Just as Kayla was about to grab a snack, Bryans boss, Alex came around the corner.

"Hey, Alex. What a pleasant surprise. Bryan is conscious and would be happy to see you."

"Hello, Kayla," he responded, walking over to meet her friendly embrace. "How have you been?"

"It's definitely been scary, but Bryan is like a Superhero. He is almost back to his old self already."

"That's good to hear in such a bad time. Wayne had told me about the accident early yesterday, but I knew it would be a hard time for the family, so I waited until today to see him."

"That's understandable. Bryan didn't wake up at all yesterday, so he wouldn't have known who visited him."

"This visit is definitely going to be a lot harder than I thought."

"Oh, he is actually okay. There are no scary wires or equipment hooked up to his body or anything. I mean if we weren't in a hospital you wouldn't think anything is wrong with him."

"Uhh…that's not really what I mean. I think maybe we should sit down," he said, motioning toward the chairs.

Alex seemed tense and looked slightly confused. There wasn't any enthusiasm in his voice when Kayla told him that Bryan was doing well. The entire moment was awkward.

"I'm not sure how to say this or if this is even the right time to tell Bryan the news, which is why I'm glad I caught you first," Alex said, holding his head down.

"You're not firing him, are you?"

"Oh, heavens no. Bryan is my right hand guy. I actually need him more than ever right now."

"Oh well, I guess I'm not sure if I understand what it is that you mean." Kayla said, eagerly concerned.

"There's been some type of accident, Kayla."

"What kind of accident?"

"I'm not certain about all the details, but...they found Wayne. Wayne is dead.

"Thank you for purchasing this book. I look forward to providing you with future entertainment that you will enjoy."

Be sure to check out all other parts of this series in addition to other books and guides.

Partially Broken Never Destroyed I
Partially Broken Never Destroyed II: Mirror Mirror
Partially Broken Never Destroyed III: The Trilogy
Partially Broken Never Destroyed IV: Unholy Matrimony
Alyce Leaves Wonderland
Experience of Life vs. Expert Advice: Relationship Guide
Hello, Guys, the Baby Has Arrived: Baby Guide
Unleashing Essential Oils: Beauty Tips
E-book Supplier for First Time Home Buyers
My Diet Your Diet Our Diet: Weight loss Guide
Little Cupcake's First Day: Children's' Book

www.imadethebook.com